# JAMES GREY

## Thirty Shades of Lust

by; Sinade Lustaer

#SinadeLustaer

www.amazon.com/author/sinadelustaer

www.twitter.com/eroticbooksread

www.instagram.com/myomanticbooksread

## CHAPTERS

1) Bedroom Secrets

2) Boy Toy

3) Dawn was her Name

## Prologue

He could sense her hunger. He could sense her fears. He could feel her deepest desires and he knew he was in too deep.

James Grey was getting used to living in Los Angeles but with Teresa missing in action, he felt a little frustrated. That soon would end when he came to the aid of a sexy woman who almost got run over by a car.

Dawn Ridgeway was stunning, in her early forties but she looked much younger, James thought. Her skin was glowing from years of taking care of herself and he knew her husband didn't appreciate her for the beauty she was. Maybe it was because of being used to the one you're sleeping with every night or maybe it was because of commitment to his successful company manufacturing airplanes.

She saw him seldom, Dawn mentioned over the cup of coffee in the early afternoon and he knew soon, she would be in his arms. But James had no idea what he was getting himself into. What the hell was it with him and older women?

Thirty Shades of Lust is the new sensational masterpiece by Sinade Lustaer.

## ** 1 **

## <u>BEDROOM SECRETS</u>

"Oh, God Yes!" She cried out again. "Make me cum! Oh, God!"

James was covered in sweat as he thrust himself deep into her. Her legs spread wide like a welcoming from months of deprivation. Her nails digging into his ass as she helped him shove his cock in as deep as it could go and James fucked her so hard he though his heart was going to explode.

He had already cum twice but she demanded more and how could he not help her get all she needed at this very moment. Her tits wobbled beneath him and her hard nipples turned him on even more as he thrust his cock in again and again until they both exploded in a remarkable orgasm.

He collapsed on top of her, his heart racing a million miles and hour as he just lay there with his face buried in the pillow. He finally looked to his side and saw her smiling satisfied as she ran her nails across his back.

"That was a good fuck."

He groaned with a smile. Words were not necessary cause she could see clearly he had a hell of a good time.

It all started that afternoon when James took his lunch break from where he worked on Avenue of the Stars in Century City, Los Angeles. He had now been in town four months and was getting better at his job with a looming possible partnership.

As head of marketing for a fashion company, he had a small team under him who did much of the social networking campaigns and magazine advertisements. He was in charge of creating winning campaigns that could reel in millions of dollars for the company. He was promised twenty percent after six months if he'd proven to skyrocket sales for Mr. Seegram.

He still didn't fuck that sexy secretary, James thought to himself as he knew she had a crush on him but he didn't wanted to jeopardize his job in any way shape or form at this early stage. Joan was her name and she loved wearing short skirts and high heels.

Quite a picture if you looked at her beneath the desk where she knew she was visible. One day James could swear she wasn't wearing any panties. He would have loved to have double checked.

He smiled as he crossed the street to the fast food restaurant he would stop by most days. James heard a sudden honking and screeching brakes of a car and saw that a woman almost got hit as she crossed the street.

"You fucking bitch!" He heard the angry driver yelling as he drove off.

James bolted to her aid and he saw she was visibly shaken.

"You okay?"

"Yes. Aggressive driver," she said as he helped her out of the street and onto the sidewalk.

"Los Angeles," James said. "They drive aggressive here."

"Thanks for helping," she smiled and James noticed the wedding ring.

She was around five foot eight in heels and stockings and dressed business casual but even so, she was quite beautiful with her long brown hair flicked sideways across her shoulder.

"I'm James."

"Dawn. You work around here?"

"Across the street." He pointed.

"Oh, I'm in this building. Just finished lunch.

"I was just gonna ask you to join me."

"I can't, but thanks."

She walked away towards her office building.

"Coffee?"

She looked back at his hopeful smile.

"I'm married."

"Coffee anyway?"

She stopped and looked at him like she was summing him up.

'He was quite handsome,' she thought. 'Tall and seemed well mannered. Not the kind of guy who would just mess around. Well, maybe… he did help her. That was nice.'

"Meet me at five, over there."

He looked at the coffee shop she was pointing at. It was next to the fast food place he was heading towards now.

"You got it." He winked.

She smiled and walked off.


He sat quietly looking across the green grass as many people where coming from lunch or on heir way. Century City was a very high-end metropolis in Los Angeles bordering Beverly Hills. This high-rise jungle was comprised of some super wealthy individuals, lawyers, bankers, movie companies, doctors and more. It was probably the richest most condensed four square miles in all of Los Angeles.

Needless to mention, he didn't think he could get bored here, James thought and suddenly he remembered Teresa. He hadn't seen her in two weeks. They sure had some incredible sex but he got busy and she got busy…

'Hi, sexy. Just thinking of you,' he texted her. 'We hadn't talked in a while. Maybe we can get together.'

James passed the secretary in the front lobby and he only smiled at her as she was speaking on the phone. She smiled back at him and he could see her short skirt close to her crotch beneath the glass of her desk.

'Maybe, maybe, maybe,' he though to himself as he entered his office. 'Maybe one day.'

"James, let's have a quick meeting," Mr. Seegram commanded as he stuck his head into James office and motioned with his hand to follow him.

James followed his boss, slash, soon-to-be-partner, into his office.

Mr. Seegram took seat behind his mahogany desk and his corner office had a fantastic view over Century City and across the large gold course that bordered the Beverly Hilton Hotel.

This was the very hotel where they held the Golden Globe Awards every year and James thought he might even get a chance one day to be invited or maybe even crash it. He had read in the past of people who snuck into the Golden Globe Awards. They met movies stars and had an incredibly good time with all the free food and alcohol imaginable. Apparently it was "THE" Party to be at.

He was in Hollywood. You never knew what could happen.

"I want you to create a campaign on our new line of wedding dresses."

Mr. Seegram handed him a brochure or some amazing wedding gowns with stunning models who fashioned them.

"Beautiful models," James mentioned.

"Look at the dresses, James. Not the sexy girls." Mr. Seegram smiled.

"I know." He smiled back as he was perusing the new line.

The meeting went on for about thirty minutes but James had a hard time focusing. His thoughts were with Dawn. The woman he was about to meet at five pm. She was married, so he didn't have much as afar as expectations. Maybe he could be a good friend. He felt a connection with her. He didn't always had to fuck a girl.

He could have female friends without having to have

sex with them. It was a nice thought.

## ** 2 **

### <u>BOY TOY</u>

It was almost five in the afternoon when James found a cozy corner in the coffee shop. He thought he'd be early incase the place was busy and he had to wait for a table but there weren't many people. He didn't order coffee yet. He wanted to wait for Dawn.

He had some time to go through some of his emails and texts and was surprised he had not heard from Teresa. That was surprising. She normally got back to him when he texted. Maybe she was mad that he had not made and effort to see her for two weeks.

"Hello there."

He looked up and saw Dawn.

"Oh, hi."

"You're early."

"A bad habit."

"I think it's a good habit." She sat down an asked, "Coffee?"

"Oh, yes, " James remembered. "I'll grab it. What do you like?"

"Ice mocha."

"Sounds good."

Dawn watched his stride as he walked to the counter to order.

'Nice ass,' she thought and heard a ping on her phone.

It was her husband Rick.

'Hi, honey. I'll be late tonight. Got some issues with this new design we're working on and the company needs the final drawings in the morning, so I have to grind it out with the crew.'

'Again,' Dawn thought. 'His company was everything. She was always last on the list. Oh well. She was used to it.'

"Here we are."

James handed her a large mocha.

"Thanks." She smiled. "That's all you're having?"

She was pointing at his large hot coffee.

"Plain old coffee. I'm a boring guy."

"I don't think so."

"You don't." He sipped.

"Well maybe you are, I don't know."

They smiled.

"Why did you ask me for coffee?" She asked and there was a pause.

"I don't know. Guess I like you."

"I'm married." She flashed her wedding band at hm.

"I saw." He hesitated while sipping from the mug. "Long time?"

"Ten years.

"Happy?"

"Guess so."

She smiled as she leaned back a little more making herself comfortable.

James noticed the beautiful lines around her mouth and how well she wore her perfectly applied lipstick. It was a light purple and matched her eye shadow.

"I like purple."

"Purple?" She asked confused."

He pointed. "Your lipstick."

"Oh, yeah me too. Ever since I was a child,

purple was always one of my favorites, and red."

"I like red," James replied. "The color of

romance."

"Oh, really?" She seemed amused.

James couldn't help but noticing her full breasts

and he couldn't help but appreciate them them with his

eyes for a moment.

She caught him.

"So, are you a boy toy?"

"Boy toy?" He laughed. "Hell no. I'm a boring

marketing guy."

He handed her his business card and she looked

over it.

"Maybe you missed your calling."

"Really?" He asked intrigued.

She shrugged.

He thought about it. "Maybe… "

"So, tell me about you, Mr. Stranger. James."

"Not much to tell. I moved to LA five month ago or so… got this new job here in the marketing department… "

"From where?"

"Connecticut, via Chicago for a few months."

"Ooh, cold." She acted like she had a cold shiver just thinking about it.

"You're right. Why I got out of there. But I have a warm heart."

"Clever." She smiled.

"Your turn."

"What?" She asked.

"Tell me about you. Your husband."

"Oh, Rick. Hard working. Has his own company for twenty years.

"Doing what?"

"Airplanes. Design and Engineering."

"Pretty intense."

"Yes, he works a lot."

"Feel deprived?" He asked jokingly.

"You're very forward Mr. Boy Toy."

"James. You can call me James."

"James." She smiled as they sipped their coffee.

She could feel herself attracted to him. She liked his light humor.

After a moment she asked; "So, a handsome guy like you don't have a girlfriend?"

"I don't look too hard. I mean. I don't like nightclubs and not often hang out in bars.

"Instead you meet women who are almost run over by cars," she added.

"Yes. That sounds more heroic."

"I like that. Heroic. You are a hero. At least today."

For a moment they gazed deep into each other's eyes and James thought he recognized her invitation.

"Can I take you home?" He asked out of the blue. He couldn't control the urge inside him.

"Not today." She smiled. Stood up and gave him a subtle look, like, 'maybe next time.'

Playfully, she waved at him and walked away.

James felt himself getting hard in his pants.

'Dammit, she was sexy. Fuck…' his mind was racing wild.

This crazy sexy feeling just came over him and he knew he wanted her in his bed, day and fucking night.

He was rushing home, horny as fuck. He felt like jacking off just thinking of her mouth on him. James instinctively rubbed over his hardon that had formed a huge bulge in his pants.

***

He eyed himself in the mirror as he was jacking off. All he could think about was Dawn. He could see her sexy lips smiling when she asked…

'Are you a Boy Toy?'

Was that a hint?

James was naked and his well-formed chest was heaving as he massaged his hard penis. He could just imagine kissing those beautiful purple lips and he could almost feel her lips going down on him. He was throbbing now as he jerked his cock harder until he ejaculated into the washing basin.

Out of breath, he leaned over the basin, caressing his balls. Since when did he become so sexualized? He wondered. He didn't always think so much about sex. What the hell are these women doing to him?

Time had slipped by and it was now almost ten pm., as James lay in bed watching a movie on TV. He didn't watch too many movies. It bored him, but this one was not too bad, starring Al Pacino and Christopher Walkin, two of his favorite actors.

'They were getting quite old now,' James thought but they were always entertaining to watch.

He looked at his phone, expecting to see a text from Teresa but nothing yet.

"Fuck." He felt frustrated.

His phone rang. It was his mother.

"Hi mom." He answered lazily.

"James, are you okay? We haven't heard from you."

"It's only been a week mother… I'm fine."

"How is LA?"

"Ah, not too boring. Work is going on…"

"You like the office?"

"Yes, mom, it's not bad."

'Mothers always worry,' James thought to himself…

***

Dawn was lying back in her bathtub with a glass of wine. Her long legs stretched out all the way as she could feel the foam bubbles tickling her skin. Rick was still working and her mind was on James. Her toenails were painted purple as well and she wondered what James would think of them. Would he find her toes sexy? Was he a toe guy? She wiggled her toes and they felt sexy and relaxing.

She felt a knot in her stomach ever since she met James. She felt excited but uneasy at the same time. She knew what was coming. It was inevitable and she was not the kind of woman who had ever cheated on her husband but Rick hadn't made love to her in a month. She sometimes wondered if he was fucking someone else. She knew he was extremely jealous and could be possessive at times, but what the fuck did he wanted her to do if he was always working.

Last time he wanted to fuck her he couldn't even get a hardon. He was too damn tired and she had to go and masturbate. It was frustrating and she felt forced to buy herself a vibrator. Rick didn't know about it, but she found a new friend. It was a fitting substitute for the time being but now she met James and it sure felt tempting. A penis rather than a vibrator could do a world of wonders to her.

Why did she have to meet James today? Was that a sign? She always resisted any involvement with another man but at the same time she felt so attracted to James that she could just fuck him in a heartbeat.

Her mind went back and forth and she could feel the inner struggle inside her very soul.

'A struggle between good and bad,' she almost whispered out loudly and Dawn smiled at the notion.

Good girl versus bad girl. What would she be? She was trying to be a faithful wife but how fucking long can you go without some affection and where was the line I the sand? Being married for ten years was a long time and she could now not even imagine having to stay in this relationship for another ten years unless something changed dramatically.

Maybe if Rick started fucking her three times a week, maybe a day would be better, but it would definitely change things. After all, that's what they did in the beginning of their relationship. They fucked everywhere. In the car, in the park, by a river stream and everywhere they could. Rick was a little younger than her and he was damn hot at the time. They were very sexually attracted to one another and got married only three months after they started dating.

Rick could not keep his hands off of he, and dammit, he fucking knows how much she likes her pussy eaten and the son of a bitch had not done it in a long time.

So what the fuck does Rick want her to do? Stay faithful and die of boredom?


Dawn lay back on the silky sheets, her naked body towel dried and she lightly touched her clitoris. Her pussy felt hot from the hot bath and she was horny. She could feel her pussy getting wet just by the mere though of a cock sliding into her. Dawn reached for her secret vibrator, the friend, Rick had no idea about and she turned it on. It vibrated in her hand and she lowered it to the opening of her vagina.

Tempting, teasing, and then she slipped it in while she was caressing her clit. "Oh... fuck... yes!"

She pushed the vibrator in and out feeling her stomach turning inside out and her clit getting harder and she curled her toes.

She wondered how James would feel inside her. Did he have a big cock? Did he shave his balls? He looked so strong and she could imagining him putting his hands around her hot ass and just fucking her deep...

"Ohhh... "

Her body curled as she fucked herself with the vibrator until she exploded. Dawn drifted of to sleep.

## ** 3 **

### <u>DAWN WAS HER NAME</u>

James heard his phone ring on his way to work.

He was sitting in morning traffic when he answered.

"Hello."

"James, It's Teresa."

"Oh, his stranger."

'Finally', he thought surprised but somehow he wished it was Dawn calling him for some strange reason.

He should be excited that to hear from Teresa, finally getting back to him, but James didn't feel too elated.

"I'm sorry I didn't get back to you," he heard her apologetic voice. "I had to go back home for a while.

"I was wondering what happened? I tried to reach you."

"I know, I'm sorry. My dad had passed away."

"What?" This was a shock to James.

"Why didn't you tell me?"

"Oh, I didn't wanted to burden you with my grief."

James suddenly felt a deep empathy towards her and all his feelings about not caring much about her faded.

"Teresa, I am so sorry."

How considering of her not to bother him with such a loss. He was shocked and felt a little emotional.

'Beyond his understanding,' James thought. 'How graceful of her.'

"Thanks," she said appreciatively.

There was a moment while James' mind was racing. He felt terrible that he was so selfish.

"If you want to get together soon," Teresa continued… "let me know."

"I will. For sure. Absolutely."


All morning James struggled with his emotions, now torn between Teresa and his new crush, Dawn. Again, he thought of how selfish he was, to not even worry that Teresa could have had something like this happen to her. His mind was on sex when there was something much more serious going on and disliked himself for a moment. He felt that Teresa didn't deserve him.

What was he to do now?

Lunchtime had already passed when James got the text from Dawn. He had been pondering what to do now and if he should meet Teresa that night. Now here was the text he had been longing for. In his face and he felt tormented as he read her text.

'Can you meet me tonight?'

'Should he feel guilty?' James thought to himself as he was driving towards the location where Dawn asked him to meet her.

Even though he felt excited, Teresa was in the back of his mind and his heart went out to her. He knew he had to shake off this feeling of guilt, after all, how was he to know…

'I'll see her tomorrow night,' James thought to himself. 'I'll make it up to her.'

Right now he had Dawn on his mind and this sexy woman was just fucking with his brain and he could not think straight.

He met Dawn at the park in Beverly Hills where she sat on a bench as the sun was setting. She had her hair up and there was something about her that felt electric. Different than from what he felt with her before. Almost like she was Colt .45 Revolver, cocked and ready to fire.

"There you are," she greeted him.

Here eyes were locked on him and James noticed her open shoes and the purple shade on her toenails. He felt a feeling of electricity running up his spine.

"Hello there," James smiled and sat down beside her. "How was our day?"

"Awe, nothing too exciting. Just work."

James couldn't help himself but leaned over and gave her a light kiss on the cheek.

"You look amazing."

"Really?" She asked.

She could see his eyes gazing into her soul. Like a beast and she felt that warm feeling in her stomach she had felt the day before, but stronger this time.

'God, she could fuck him right here on the bench,' she thought and almost giggled that her mind was thinking such dirty thoughts.

How bad of her? She was playing a mind game with herself and she enjoyed it thoroughly. Boy, it was about time she felt alive again.

"So, where do you live?" She asked and he looked at her a little surprised.

"Not too far."

He stood up like a man who realized his mission and he took control of the situation as he pointed her in the direction of his car.

They were on the second floor of the building and Dawn followed him toward the door of his apartment. She could feel the excitement growing inside her with every step, like butterflies were fluttering into her soul. Dawn knew this was the day she would be an unfaithful wife and there was nothing that could stop it.

"Make yourself at home." James gestured towards the couch after he shut the door behind her.

She sat down.

"Want something to drink?" He asked.

"Something strong."

She was a little nervous after all. The future was uncertain except for this very moment.

James poured them each a bourbon and handed her a glass as he sat down beside her. He could smell her perfume and it excited him. For the moment he had forgotten Teresa as he relaxed back into the couch, taking a sip.

"Mmm, tastes good," Dawn said, savoring the taste of the strong liquor.

James just smiled at her and after a moment he lightly touched her hand.

"How long has it been?"

"I haven't had a strong drink in a few weeks... " she started.

"I mean... since you've been with another guy?"

His hand folded more firmly around her now and he could feel a light tremble as they gazed into one another's eyes.

"Not since I've been married… ten years…"

His lips moved closer to hers and she hesitated, just for a moment, then she kissed him. Stronger and stronger their kiss grew and Dawn felt herself becoming overwhelmed with sexual energy.

James' lips moved down her neck and she tensed as his hand moved into her bra, caressing her hard nipple. Then slowly his tongue touched her nipple and it was shocking. Electrifying and she grabbed him tighter. He sucked harder on her nipple could explode. Her pussy was becoming moist and warm.

"James… " It was a loud whisper…

She didn't even recognize her own voice. She felt like a tigress in heat and her voice felt like the growl of an animal.

Dawn guided his hand into her wet panties and his strength grew as he pulled them down her smooth legs.

Dawn wanted to take off her heels but he stopped her.

"No. Leave them…"

He took off her panties and opened her legs a little as he went down on his knees. She smelled so good and he wanted to taste her on his tongue. James pushed her back as he moved his mouth into her crotch and started licking her clit.

"Oh, God… " She squirmed and her body tensed.

He stuck his finger into her now very wet pussy and he sucked her clit harder. She wanted to just explode as her hand reached for his hard cock. She unzipped his pants and trying to get her mouth to it they both tumbled onto the carpet.

Her mouth found his hard cock and she started sucking it as hard a she could and it felt sooo fucking good that it was shocking to her. Shocking because she had not sucked on another mans penis in more than ten years. They rolled into sixty-nine position and he was eating her out as she tried to get his big cock all the way down her throat. She almost chocked but then tried again got better at it quickly.

Dawn could not remember when last she felt this excited.


They were covered in sweat now and he was inside her like a perfect fitting shaft.

"Oh, God Yes!" She cried out again. "Make me cum! Oh, God!"

They were on his bed and he thrust himself deep into her. Her legs opened up as far as they could. Her nails digging into his ass, helping him get his cock in as deep as it could go.

Her mind was in a different stratosphere and all that mattered was this moment of pure climactic bliss.

James ejaculated for the second time on top of her and big sigh escaped his beast-like physique and then he rolled over and off of her.

Dawn only hesitate for a moment, then took his cock in her mouth sucked it again. She wasn't gong to let this moment of magic slip away.

"Oh no, I can't take it," he cried but she didn't stop.

"Come on, bad boy!"

She sucked him till he was ready again. Her tits wobbled beneath him and her hard nipples turned him on even more as he thrust his cock in again and again until they both exploded in a remarkable orgasm.

They collapsed together and he lay still on top off her. She felt she couldn't breathe and his heart was beating so loud it felt like it was inside her chest.

She pushed him off of her and he lay there with his face buried in the pillow. He finally looked to his side and saw her smiling satisfied as she ran her nails across his back.

"Okay?" She asked.

"Better than okay." He smiled.

James knew this was not the last he wanted of her.

'Wow,' Dawn thought to herself as she was cherishing this moment of pure magic.

How was it even possible that she had missed out on so much for so damn long? Rick was now only a vague memory. Not in a very long time had she felt this relaxed, this excited, and this ready to take on the world.

She kissed him lightly on his lips. Is eyes were shut but seeing the light smile on his lips made her feel appreciated.

"Dawn..." he whispered.

She felt good.

THE END


\#SinadeLustaer

www.amazon.com/author/sinadelustaer

www.twitter.com/eroticbooksread

www.instagram.com/myomanticbooksread

www.pinterest.com/eroticbooksread

James Grey. Thirty Shades of Lust by Sinade Lustaer.

www.ingramcontent.com/pod-product-compliance
Lightning Source LLC
Chambersburg PA
CBHW071458150726
48000CB00006B/2606